Cold Flushes

– Stride –

By the same author:

Snowfruit (Taxus Press)
Dusting Round The Jelly (Odyssey)

Cold Flushes
Mary Maher

Cold Flushes
First edition 1994
© Mary Maher 1994
All rights reserved

ISBN 1 873012 79 9 *(paperback)*
ISBN 1 873012 80 2 *(hardback)*

Cover illustration
© Pam Doran 1994
Design by Joe Pieczenko

Acknowledgements
Staple, Otter, Illuminations, Smiths Knoll, Spectrum, Bogg, Bare Bones, Frogmore Papers, Poetry Nottingham, Issue One, Smoke, Envoi, Working Titles, The Social Worker, Memes, Iota, Bound Spiral, Hybrid, Various Artists, The North, Ramraid Extraordinaire, Poetry Durham, The Rialto, Exile, Pennine Platform, Odyssey, Tandem, Scratch, Headlock, Avon Intelligencer, Terrible Work
and *Uncompromising Positions.*

Published by
Stride Publications
11 Sylvan Road, Exeter
Devon EX4 6EW

CONTENTS

Tidal Mouth 7
Hand Washing His Shirt 8
The Most Intimate Touch 9
Study 10
My Heart And Eye 11
Impotence 12
Friends 13
The Tiger-Skin Rug 14
Over The Top 15
Seal 16
Not Winchester 17
Oasis 18
The Light Of St. Ives 20
The Tapdancer 21
Reading After Dark 22
Seeing In The Rain 23
Harmony 24
Re-membering The Dance 25
Umbrellas To Spare 26
The Small School 27
Being Creative 28
Pulling The Chain 29
I've Been Wanting 30
A Poor Bond 31
Bedsit 33
Red Hot Pokers 35
Dream Of Superiority, A Little Racist 36
Alice And Mussolini 37
Spirit 38
Accommodating Alice 39
Looking For A Laugh 41
End Of Season 42
Threat 43
The Door Into Intensive Care 44
Afterwards 45
Grass And Banks 46
Rural Echoes 47
After The First Sharp Breath 48
Come-Back 49

She Tells A Bedtime Story 50
Half Of It 52
She Loves A Monk 53
Did He Ever Dream 54
Hepworth 55
Gwen John Isn't Sitting 57
A Letter To Daniela Crasnaru, Romania 58
deaf-blind girls 60
Country Dancer 61
Candy Looks For Herself 62
Candy Snaps 63
Candy And The Slow Cooker 64
The Lawful Position Of Coal 66
That Bomb Inside Us Cruises L.A. April 92 67
Mantelpieces 68
June 69
The Outside Pool 70
Uncommitted 71
Duchamp's Urinal 1917 72
Women's Platform 73
Researching Uncertain Ground, Stanpit Marsh 74
Sitting On The Map 75
Trailers 77
Stockpiling 79
Being On A Ring Road 80
Blue Gnome 81
On The Road To Abersoch, Election Eve 1992 82
High Tide 84

TIDAL MOUTH

Nowadays
the great log
in our river
is a familiar sight;

and the black seabird
perched on it
looking towards
the swimming pool roof.

A long time ago
the tree
swept down the Taw
in a gale.

It was low tide
when it reached
the estuary
and town bridge.

Here it lay
in the sand and
very rhythmically
began to root

until no tide
could budge it.

HAND WASHING HIS SHIRT

She immerses the toughened collar,
lets her hands dabble with it.
A few minutes to merge with the window,
distance, the water.

She squeezes and lifts the shirt free
of the water, feels it drag.
Where she has wiped vermilion and cobalt
is stubbornness

and now that the grey has gone,
brilliance.
She goes out into the glare of the sun
and shakes his shirt.

Its ripples cascade from father to daughter
and again
from rough struggle between the shoulders
to fine art at her wrists.

THE MOST INTIMATE TOUCH

came when it was over.

After the hikes,
the long talks exploring night and day,
meals with wine by candlelight,
log fires, good sex, flames,
gazing over bays,
towards sunrise

we stood
side by side watching a kettle
our new lives not about
and you put an arm
around me
pressure
and release just right.

STUDY

Piles of paper around the edge
of a spacious mahogany table:
several marked urgent in red.
He's cycled to work. She sits
at his table drinking coffee – decaff.
Touches his pens, rubbers, clips.
Reads little yellow memos stuck
to a coppr jug filled
with dried honesty: Ring
Daisy, Copeland, Barbara.
Outside a silver birch
shivers and sways.
The pavement is wet.
How he fills the quietness of his room!
And then he phones. Is she O.K.?
Can she find everything she needs?
This is what he'll say.
But she lets it ring.
Likes to hear its after-throb
penetrate silence.

MY HEART AND EYE

I woke saying:
blindness is a patch on the heart –
a morning flush; and can't deny
I was rather pleased.

Now round my neck hangs
a locket: an image
heartshaped and plump,
stuck with a bit of pink plaster.

That's the picture
but what's the use?

To love you with all my heart
when it can't see what it's doing?
To think positive and whip off the plaster?
What and risk bleeding to death in the gutter?

But if sightfree I were
to float in the shallows of your eye,
wear wings in your ear
and tread water on your tongue

I don't think
my heart would sink.

IMPOTENCE

Over gurgles from the jacuzzi
Jack heard his wife
let in the travelling man,
flirt to her heart's content.

She'd ordered
a mop and bucket,
a yellow duster
'to bring sunshine to our days'.

In the years when she'd
been lithe and eager
she'd loved the hardware stores
up Blackpool Hill:
nails by the pound,
hammers, screws,
the criss-cross stubble
of metal files;
the foundry smell.

Now she softened
the Kleeneze man
into confessing
he'd been made redundant,
once had been a major.
'Oh major sad, major laugh,' she sang.

Upstairs
in the bathroom
sadness swirled
for the fellow down below.
Jack knew that need
to penetrate another's life,
make something happen
since she'd been
made strange and sweetly whole
on the women's ward.

FRIENDS

There are Antlers For Sale
in the lean to
by the church.
The Hunt's been through.
The path's churned up.
So's she
but he
unwraps a laugh
around her like the moss
he later peels from trunks
fallen in the January gale.
'Chicken meat,' he calls
pointing to the white wood
underneath.
She stands upright
as thin winter trees.
Watches him bend.

In the evening on tv
plane crash survivors
of 72 in Uruguay
discuss life in the snow
40 below, the dead,
their strangest meal.
How they dined on wine and chocolate
before they started on their friends.
Back home, how they coped.
She looks on,
intense,
declares to the sitting room
that this rare union
must be some form of sacrament.

An act of friendship, he says
steadying her gaze
through banisters
as he goes for a bath
before the programme ends.

THE TIGER-SKIN RUG

Sighted when thirsty.
Shouldered, crated, ferried
back to the family seat.
Skin lingers on.

Terminally shocked.
Unswallowed dust
clogged in his throat,
growl yellow.

Any incomer's eye he catches
from that barrel on safari
to a peep
round the door
of an English drawing room.
South-facing.

Trodden on,
head – a footstool
or a little stage
to assert the young heir of the house.

The bagger's dead.
Generations ago.
And buried.

On the other side of life
skin has
no stomach for tinkling ivories
after dinner,
wildlife on tv,
a game of Trivial Pursuit;

but outlives each heartful of yawns,
lets dying firelight
tease out gold in stripes,
keeps an open mouth.

OVER THE TOP

Along a lane which runs high
over the moors, my mood changes up.

I drive back across this county
and there is life in the dead of night.

A wild recall; wildness reaching out:
a violin veers from the tape deck,

Leonard Cohen storms, 'First
we'll take Manhattan, then we'll take Berlin'.

There's a fox in the road.
In another second I'm calling

'I love you' as he just misses my wheels,
swallows me whole with his eyes.

Crazy joy wriggles out of my heart
and on through the hedgerows.

SEAL

Once a week we leave
our separate places
to meet where
fluent rain
transparent
on the windows
often seals us
for days to come
in each other's face.

NOT WINCHESTER

She can't take new love just anywhere.

This path, that gate,
this seat, her ex,
his walk, his kids,
not her new love's.

She can't take new love just anywhere

because old ones
past but not remains
won't lie down
with Norman bones.

You can't take new love just anywhere.

Self-conscious city
used to digs: 'Evidence
of tapeworms found
in medieval sewer site.'

You see you can't take new love just anywhere.

Around the Buttercross,
through the Close,
across the Water Meadows,
up St. Catherine's Hill

taking her new love to see the sights

slippery paths unwind
skeletal stuff to eyeball
new bypass supporters,
modern hillfort fighters.

Her new love has a bone to pick with Winchester.

OASIS

One day   he goes to St. Ives   for two days.
He wants a holiday from other people's thirsts
and is going to meet a literary lady of mature years.

Their letters have often collided in the post.

In the flesh they avoid one another   slightly.

      Their behaviour is painterly;

      light and moving slowly
      as a new colour in water.

Before an abstract

      (Bob Devereux's 'The New Beginning')
      at the Orion

      in terms of balance
      a hug comes naturally.

      His leather jacket creaks.
      The floorboards creak.

Out on the road again
a bare foot on the accelerator
swivels to the brake
downhill to the quay at Lamorna.

      He picks heaps of daffodils.

      The sea claps.

When the literary lady
crouches in the little bookshop
a framed portrait of Virginia Woolf
falls on her head.
He kisses it better.

At dusk they go to Madron.
The relief,
        after they ease their bodies
                through the stone circle

        is phenomenal.

On the second day they reflect on the creamy sand.
In white, adored by the sun, they gather inkspots
                on their feet.

THE LIGHT OF ST. IVES

There it is
taking a dip
hundreds and thousands of dips
flushing out waves.

And the sand
a split and laid back apricot
sucking a sun bone dry:

a light echo in the sky.

THE TAPDANCER

leaves the smile on my face.

When he's not in work
it's hand to mouth in swingtime.
Flicking kicks
hips get looser
we get closer.

And you don't need a thing,
can do it anywhere.
O.K. shoes
could be a problem.
But outside, in the rain
voting with your feet
on the streets
is musical.
Flick. Kick.
Try it on a corner and they're
looking for a jingling cap.
Use an umbrella
you've got a roof over your head.

Side together back,
solo spots,
give you time
to put your best foot forward;

a foot you could cock your ear to.

READING AFTER DARK

Once blind
Jesse puts away his braille

and with a guide
follows black pin men

walking on white paper;
this-that this-that.

Jesse sees unhooded words
take off across the land

like hawks, their power
unleashed from keepers' wrists.

Knowing darkness
he sees more than most.

Last night for instance he saw
3 streetwise men strolling

in long black coats,
shoulders close and the spaces

between their necks,
white flashing lights.

Dreams are open eyes.
Waking these mornings,

something else.

SEEING IN THE RAIN

Rain chips the sea

and St. Ives rises
above a fizz
of harbour lights.

Ochre settles on roofs.

We see the blindman.

Fore Street's shining wet.
It feels good
to be back
splashing in the gutter.

His white stick
is coming around
the corner again
divining cobbles:
each step secured in a smile
– a smile so close
it mesmerises

and then he says
'I can see
someone else loves the rain.'

HARMONY

I heard over the radio
that he'd left, taking only
a tin trunk of books,
a clay water pot
and an umbrella.

I followed him
fascinated by
his bare, articulate feet
treading dust along the road.

Two boys hurried behind
carrying the tin trunk
and chattering
nineteen to the dozen.

When it began to rain
he gave them money
to shush
and opened up
his black and white
striped umbrella.

RE-MEMBERING THE DANCE

in a howling storm
did you ever go
to the window
and watch legs
scatter scattering
the words of a wise old girl

them's wild
with wind under their tails m'dear

and did you ever
toss and toss
in your pretty village bed
and dream of the local christian-girl
made-saint
whose legs were harvested
instead of corn

pinnacles fell from her church
right through her nave
last year

and do you ever whine
you've had a shower put in
and got a water butt
for god's sake
then fret
about your old neighbour
who's neither indoor lavatory
nor bath

and you know she sleeps
like a baby
to a roofslate slither

have you ever danced for rain
has it ever been that bad
when an english obsession
with weather's sane

UMBRELLAS TO SPARE

I'm left with them.
A dozen; the stubby, the elegant, dull and erotic
hang on the hooks in my hall.
Friends seem prepared for falling rain but not for when it stops.

I haven't an umbrella of my own
but if I were to choose, it would have to be the elegant one;
the black silk roof of a
romantically grieving folly with transparently tearful walls.

I'd practise
putting it up after that first sign, a rainspot on the cheek;
swing it like a promising stick
with a point that when raised would prick wild skies.

Then I'd fancy inviting over
eleven forgetful owners, for rain.
We'd wave a fleet of upturned brollies off
feted by leaves falling for the occasion.

A regatta would rock,
a lane flow, and we'd get essentially drenched
while somewhere an elegant lady would pout
by a weeping window, like a dry erogenous zone.

THE SMALL SCHOOL

The clock ticks on till lunchtime.
The headmaster is worried about dinner scraps
and goes for buckets.
His wife the teacher is livid with talking children
and asks him for the cane.

In the playground their son is chasing
the girl who beat him at maths.
He won't ask her to marry him today
but pushes her into the girls' lavs
and tells her he didn't miss her
when she had mumps. No one missed her.
She cannot believe this. She'll remember this
for the rest of her life;
see him standing there in his khaki shorts,
no shirt, no socks.

Her mum says he's got a plum in his mouth.

The others are gathering round the dark shed
where silver wheels, spades and forks glint.
'It is serious,' she hears the headmaster say
so she starts to walk over trying not to hurry
to be near something serious. She feels happy.
It is Alan with a fork through his foot.

Her thumb is inky and the sun shines on her desk.

'Go for the cane.'

The headmaster is standing in the playground
worrying about drainpipes and talking to himself.
The girl likes looking up at the sky with him.
She feels close to rain.

BEING CREATIVE

They search for a torch.
Flick it on
and their faces are eclipsed.
Up the hill
away from the longhouse
they call to shooting stars
and stop to pat waxed pockets
as if their contents,
gingernuts and flasks of tea
are snug secrets needing reminders
about the forthcoming sunrise.
It's been a pretty creative week:
high but in control.
Output, good. And lovebites too
from the new girls.
Enough to warrant scarves
and this sudden urge
to see the sun come up.
Be there. A new day.
But as the moon fades
a white mist rolls
over the longhouse in the valley
and up the hill towards them.
They stare in disbelief.

PULLING THE CHAIN

We often walk through the water meadows
from St. Cross to Kingsgate by the River Itchen.
In April if you're overdue
I'll run along the towpath
in my huge fisherman's jersey.

Miss Bishop, a retired officer from Queen Alexander's Corps,
the owner of our flat and proud of her loneness
doesn't mind if I'm sick in the night.
Pulling the chain
is a sign of life she says.

While you were kicking this morning
Miss Bishop danced
as she shook
her hand-hooked rugs
where the stone rabbit peeps
between the rosemary and sprouts.
When she saw me looking
she shied away with,
'I came up on the horses today.'

Will you ever show your face?
I've started doing giant crosswords.
9 DOWN: Element snaps (6,5).
Waters Break? Now apparently
you're standing on your head,
it's engaged they say.
I wonder how you feel
suspended within a hair's breadth
of my bone circle.

Miss Bishop's out there picking
a bunch of forced rhubarb.

I'VE BEEN WANTING

You were wearing your hair up
and raindrop earrings.
Your ears are lovely.
I've been wanting to tell you
for a long time

ever since that sultry afternoon
when strange eyes accused,
'You don't want to push do you?'
and put me out.

They hoicked me up groggy
and dangled a daughter
before me.

'Warra bloody thing,' I gibbered
then saw your ears.

A POOR BOND

It's been 25 hours
so far.
Where are you?
Where's my water?
They're all crying in here.
I haven't seen you properly yet.
Don't you care?
You might be tired but I am tired too.
Bloody tired. I need you.
I know you don't know which cry is mine
but it might be any cry you hear.
Aren't you worried?
You cut the cord.
But this is going too far.
Say to the midwife
I want to see my baby
and if she doesn't do exactly what you want
kick her guts out
or I'll scream your house down.

I can feel a condition
in the crook of your arm:
You will love me
if I stop crying.
That's why I'm crying.

Oh how you love
this blue honeycomb blanket.
You lay me on it smiling.
First you bring one side over
and then the other.
So tight.
Criss-cross-criss-I'm-your-little-mummy.
Now my arms can't wave.
My legs can't go.
How safe you feel.

I'm growing.
Up!

I'm running
my arms flung wide.
Wind billows my coat.
I'm flying to you.
That's right. Crouch.
Sit on those heels of yours.
Arms open.
We're on a par.
Do you think
you could handle love
at this level,
see how I feel?

BEDSIT

I think reality
is back working in the shop
meeting people
and selling things

like chocolate
and drink

no chocolate's not
reality
it's a substitute
for love the tele said
and drink
        for feeling things

I met him
in the shop didn't I
he came in for a copy
of the MIRROR and HELLO
and now we've got this lovely baby
who keeps crying

and she doesn't want a drink

and he's still out there
meeting people
and mending things

and I want to throw her
out of the window
the green buds are lovely out there

but I lay her on the rug
and look at her
she's quieter now
so I cry a little

I think it's relief really

and it's not his fault
he's out there mending things

RED HOT POKERS

Molten spears,
quiet warriors rising
every year.
Their shadows hatch
on our neighbour's
whitened wall.

Thunder-mouth June, the wipe-out
of cuckoos
and in the curtained dawn we remember
how we used to cup our ears
before we learned to panic
puzzling out the difference
between the beginning and the end
before we started to run as I did once
thinking I heard my daughter
screaming in the lane. I could have killed
until I turned the corner and saw her hysterical
with laughter and I could breathe again
and walk on sharing her imaginary friends in trees.

DREAM OF SUPERIORITY, A LITTLE RACIST

And he
was running
in the streets.

And he was 5 weeks old.
And you spurted
after him with milk.

And we summoned the media
to our little room
to witness our phenomenon.

Meanwhile it came to the attention
of some Japanese men
who called an audience

to the assembly line
and there they hummed patiently
in little black business suits

for a 5 week old wrestler
to come running with a shadow
and a rubber mat.

And a sumo baby came
followed
by our little one

and we
in the English room
were aghast.

ALICE AND MUSSOLINI

It would be irrelevant
to say He's dead
when Alice brings up
Billy in the present tense.

A photo of him blushing
in his coffin
graces the whisky
on the sideboard.

Alice misses him;
particularly in Tescos
where he used to
push her trolley

but she never would've married
she tells the check-out girl
for the umpteenth time, if Mussolini
had not invaded Ethiopia.

On standby
Billy said
he might not come back.
In the event he didn't even go

and paid for years:
a lover of war films
and flying black hair
rallying to Alice's charge.

When he finally went
he left a wife and daughter
at odds, sipping whisky
spiked with orange.

SPIRIT

Somewhere in the United States
are photographs of a basketball team
taken outside a pub on the River Thames.
Tall, black blazered men, enormous grins
and pints.

In the middle
a tiny woman
gloved and flirting.
Double whisky
in one hand.

Easy with strangers all her life, that day
she tapped their arms with happiness.

Drink finished and goodbyes said we then
continued on our journey to the hospital
and I was glad I went into the room first.
Had time to warn her: it won't be long.
She stood exposed in silence before
the black hole that was his mouth
waiting for the shutter.

ACCOMMODATING ALICE

I am lying
on Alice's bed; a single bed

in a sheltered bungalow
under a spreading willow

and looking at the red emergency cord
taped to the wall.

Alice is worried
about pulling it accidentally.

Janet the warden has just
buzzed through on the intercom:

not to chat particularly
but to see if Alice can.

Alice still can and wants to
but Janet's not too keen.

Outside it's a sunny day
so round and round the garden

go the old bones while they can;
wild rabbits graze about their feet.

Dogs and cats give no chase
because they're not allowed;

can't be properly cared for here
but a bird in a cage is O.K.

Today I've come to take Alice out.
A whisky or two

then down to the churchyard
to which she brings bedding plants

for a double grave.
'I must tend it while I'm still here,

although when I'm not here of course
I'll very definitely, *be here!*'

Alice's laugh ricochets
around the graveyard.

LOOKING FOR A LAUGH

Under the bedclothes with her niece
splitting custard creams from the NAAFI
Dot mimicked flying bosses with moustaches
and a dad she'd spoon fed to the end
and shaved after that. *Dot... Dot...*

*I'm afraid miss, you nearly made him
a bigamist* said the police officer
at her wedding.
The fiancé in the RAF had got Dot
a diamond – a solitaire; and pregnant at forty-two
so she stopped them cancelling
True Confessions from the paper shop.

Ma Ma when can we have a colour tele?
When you get your paints out son.
With his club foot he'd led his mam a pretty dance.
He hated shoes and the indoor life,
the posh advice of specialists. He grew
inside his mother's laugh
in waiting rooms with magazines.

Taking port and custard creams the niece
found her aunt at eighty-two
cooking egg and chips for Sunday lunch.
I like to eat well, Dot said
and who are you?

END OF SEASON

He was standing on the hill, deserted
by his sheep
driven to their end
like him, sensing something
but then she's
nearly there
her boot on the bottom bar
of the gate
lost under a black moon.
Everything about her points to him
across fields
and he's failing to call
through grass which grows
higher and higher.
Her feet lift
like heavy bales.
Then he sees the toes of her boots shining
through a blade of dawn
and she's a giant
against a lighter sky
leaning down
and holding him
and telling him again
her world
is on the hill.

THREAT

We trickled over the mountains
Angie's eyes catching us
as she danced between us
Once she ran to the hedge
picked a foxglove
that old heart's cure
you'd need
in a few years
She gave it to you
and you passed it on to me
She laughed
and I went on ahead
raising it high
as if it was our banner
our rabble's banner

    And then thunder

    Pounding downhill towards us from behind the hedge

    We ran neither up nor down the lane

    Played dead

and when the first horse drew alongside

our hearts took over the pounding   We continued walking

This time

I held the banner straight out in front
                              a dripping spear

THE DOOR INTO INTENSIVE CARE

Here, against the middle of this double door
is where I feel most alive.

From the ceiling to the floor
a rod
right through me.

He's in there
a single door
a 'Ring the Bell' away
on several tubes

but through this double door
there's a passage with a cushioned floor.

AFTERWARDS

Tonight the sky winds a stole
round my shoulders.

And your eyes
daft happy in star-drift
toss light after life

in images, in images, in images
of life.

GRASS AND BANKS

Ruth and Harold
were expected in the lanes
like grass and banks.

When Harold died
Ruth slung a camera
over her shoulder

and brought home
moss, snow,
leaves, light,
icicles still ringing.

Water runs through her albums.
River roots and willows steady it.

Occasionally
in a different light
a well thrown piece of litter
like a blue fertiliser bag
on a miserable day
or a gold cigarette packet
in clover
catches her eye.

RURAL ECHOES

She empties her basket
on to the trestle table
and cries.

Smoke drifts over
grassy hummocks.
Heart fire is cavernous
and silent.
Sparks party.

Fields, midsummer night;
she wanders between
house, barn, byre
untying her knot.

Dogs watch each mouthful
clownfaced children eat
then re-thread guests
in a perpetual chain.

She gets her dog Chessy, from the car.
Swears she'll disown him if he fights.
But he stays close while she sits
on a bale and rolls tobacco.
The sax rears
through the barn roof
to the stars.

Bats flit the treeline
dive into the yard.

Later her barefeet are spinning
on old grain sacks.
Chessy asleep
on her shoes
hides a nasty
leg bite.

AFTER THE FIRST SHARP BREATH

In hand-me-down black costumes
two of us sit in the shallow water
backs against the sea
and wait for the swell of a wave
calm as politeness to lift us.

The friend who brought us
to this wild bay
where water is so clear
inspite of polluted stories
waits on the stones

with the dog she says
has more God in him
than she can know
but it's because of her
we know there are

amazing mushrooms on the cliffs,
that this is fulmar
breeding ground,
the bright flower inland
is a rare corn marigold.

She looks great today
in a blue shirt and showing
the legs she has kept
hidden since her heart
was knocked back.

Tomorrow she might
roll up her sleeves,
show her arms,
come in the sea with us.
After the first sharp breath

it's truly warm.
We could tell her that.

COME-BACK

She has found
on idle days
she rises
until she is
bread

lording it over
a wafer of moon
and the hunter
who comes back
thin as a wolf
with a blunt mouth.

SHE TELLS A BEDTIME STORY

I tried not to ask,
What about me?
when you fell in love with Mrs. Butcher
on your first day at school;
not to mind
when you said I could live next door.
But it was me in the bath
on a page of your Story Book
and mine the back
you scrubbed for one of her stars.

This is a Once Upon A Time story
I can never tell.
I might frighten you with roars,
that would not matter,
but I'll not be there to cuddle you
hold you high against the sun
tickle you till tears ran dry.

Sometimes now in a haze
we are figures
holding hands, walking to the shops,
picking berries from the hedge
rolling out grey pastry
then washing up.

Each time I go under
counting one to ten
I take this picture of you
in a skyblue dress
Queen of the Castle
on a heap of builders' sand.

If I go out today
may I come back
and settle in a corner of your keep
which in time you'll forget to dust
except maybe once a year,
say spring,

then hazarding a guess I'd say
they lived happily ever after?

HALF OF IT

After somersaulting
in a womb
and sharing
a pram, a desk,
a billet in the R.A.F.
the twins separated and married.

One bloomed
only for a season
on his wife's heavenly skin.
Tucked up his knees
like he used to
and with her
flew head over heels
between stars
in fluid nights.

When she left
'to seek her own identity',
again he came to earth.

He couldn't understand.
Without him she'd
get stranded
on a city island.

Friends offered
'Being on your own
is a time of growth'.

They didn't know the half of it;

sniggered
at his stoop,
bent knees
in cellar dives
bopping under disco lights.

SHE LOVES A MONK

Picking over ruins
in a gentleman's park
is her out-of-this-world monk,
earthed hairshirt
and as he picks he chants
a song about suppression.
She draws closer
quizzing a hem
which quietly works the dew.
It fades to donkey brown
her favourite colour.
We are talking, she says, in 1993
of ordinating women.
Her monk rises to touch on
ghosts since the dissolution
and wants to do an inventory,
know where the library's gone,
if that distant hump's a stone
or a stone-robber.
At last her time has come
to sing a haunting song
because neither of them know:
Gone to limbo you and me...
She crosses his palm
with cold tears when
he sees her and asks her
...

DID HE EVER DREAM

In fact once in bed did he ever turn over
What disturbed his night
Stars crowding him, not giving him enough dark
A world made entirely of sheep
Would carpenters or their apprentices make crosses on the side
A missing tree
Always drawing the donkey with short legs
Little children with chunky crayons like spears
Being alone with God
Words. Which one was he
Tripping over someone at his feet
Birds
Pop up cacti in the desert
Thirty three
His mother cursing him for being rude
Afterwards her face
Something going wrong on Ascension day
The arms of women
Being a gardener for ever and ever

HEPWORTH

She came from Yorkshire
to hammer in
the light
of St. Ives and the landscape of her forehead
butts
bold as bronze
into the room,
smooth, shining.
And from these photographs
you can tell
she knew
the nature of her hands;

the weight of holding life,
hardness plucked
from around the heart,
a slow screwing inwards,
relating touch
and fuck.
The coming out
of fulness:
motherchild.

No angelic visitation
in the circling garden.
She abstracted space
then turned the table.

Caught in the act
Barbara has earthed time.
Stood it up

until fire came.
Now time moves on.

A bed lies unsleeping
in the summerhouse
and in the studio
a grief of dust

that never made it
nets tools.

GWEN JOHN ISN'T SITTING
for D. Woolf

Literate.
A literate woman with an enquiring mind
is that what this painting says
the gaze falling to a winged book
at her breast?

A drawn curtain anchored by a closed book
invites the light she needs

on to the table where a pen lies in wait.

She steadies herself on a glowing white cushion
in a wicker chair: willow
woven again and again by paint.

Or is Gwen saying something about the complexities
of this chair she carries from canvas to canvas?
Its vacancy groaning for missed confinements
or have her chair-days come early
or were they always with her?

Nothing so pretentious maybe;
skindeep, paintings don't talk
they just look, like us
and the book might not be literature;
it could be maps (what interior next?)
a diary (oh those important dates),
or someone else's disturbing secrets
(there is a slight 'uh' about the lady's face),
hints on household etiquette, recipes, memoranda.

I'd rather it wasn't poetry: too inward looking altogether
but of course there's no reason
why it shouldn't be a book of reproductions like this.

('A Lady Sitting' by Gwen John)

A LETTER TO
DANIELA CRASNARU,
ROMANIA

Before Ceausescu's fall
you hid poems
in a box of onions
in your aunt's cellar.
You called them Letters From Darkness.

They are lightmiracles.
Each loop a noose
a capital a head
a comma   waits
cups an ear   listens
for what's coming.

A fullstop   silence.

Your words are priceless.
Mine have an eye to loaves and fishes

have a common currency,
are used
to being spent.

Swung jostling in a shopping basket
they squabble, spill over
but I don't even bother to look back.
My shoulder's not my horizon.

Your voice –
the rasp of slippers down concrete steps,
the staying power of your earth,
onion breath.

Mine is a fat child.

Imagining walking your streets
where one word could buy
or sell my life

like a shot I hear
my old infant teacher,

'Hands together'.

And first to fall
is my agnostic pose.

deaf-blind girls

reach across
bedside lockers
in the morning
their fingers talk
into palms
lips punch
eyes shadow box

COUNTRY DANCER

Each night of the week
she sleeps against a different border.
Men in high towers watch over.
She tells the children to be quiet
when they come blinking like stars.
Silence can be a drawstring,
an old family purse or a
lit powder trail running.
A barbed spark, a face lights up,
suddenly a guard in need
of a mother remembers his life.
Day is no place for the children,
breasting the finishing tape no longer
a sport and they can't suffer in silence
until it's too late and stare into space.
The old stare at the ground, know
what's been lost except this one old woman.
Stick close. What she knows is the way back.
She twists and reaches reporters' mikes.
Her partners are those who won't listen.
There are no homes here and yet
with every step, every thrust of the chin
she's kicking you out.

CANDY LOOKS FOR HERSELF

Candy followed the usual trail to India to find herself
but didn't.
In fact she came closest when she took a look
in the deserts of Morocco, Egypt, Jordan
and latterly Kuwait.

She had done a Nanny Course
and one in Landscape and Acrylics – passed in flying colours.

Many were the hours she totted up
the different qualities of wet and dry sandplay
for her princely charges:
Look, dry sand behaves like water
and with wet you can build castles.

The truth of this was borne out
when men in a hurry on high
pissed all over the desert
so their generals could make all manner of pies.
But before this
Candy had always enough water to paint the desert.
Now her brush, dry and stiff, caught her eye.

Rumours were breaking out about uncapping the oil.
Her canvas warped temporarily coping with the depth of this news.
Candy stood, back against the porcelain chill of the sink.
The royals had gone and Kate Adie arrived, a fluent frontdrop
for chaos. Outside cacti were explosive and the sky
a furious blue, livid about its land
drove towards vanishing point taking Candy's eye with it.
But that meeting place on which she had such high hopes
was gone. The horizon was in ruins.
There was panic by the sink as her canvas split,
showed up the legs of the easel and behind it
a yellow flaking wall.

Candy's eyes welled for the sensual weight
of her sable brush before she had squeezed it.

CANDY SNAPS

High in the Cameroons
Candy is pedalling hard
when on to the road
a girl
comes dancing

raising arms
to the mountains

which spin and bind her
in rainbow sashes.

Fingers flick blue into the sun.
Feet tap an earthwise song.

Instantly Candy
reaches for her camera
then finds
she cannot do it.

Back home
each time
she tells
her story

a girl comes dancing
on to the road
raising arms
to the mountains
which spin and bind her
in rainbow sashes,
fingers flicking blue into the sun,
feet tap tapping an earthwise song.

CANDY AND THE SLOW COOKER

Any fool could use it.
All it needed
was to simmer.

A delicate surface
rippling
under the lid
covering a dish's
details.

Boiling would pock-mark
and Candy could see ugliness
like this.

She looked down
at a host of tough,
cheap cuts
subtly mixing
and shuddered as though
it were effective muscle.

Of course the slowness
ruined her day.
She lost all sense
of direction
with time to waste,
eat whenever

and simmering hints
disturbed
without pointing
to the table,
were never clear
like the current
in a crowd's behaviour
or the politeness of
'Wash your hands!'

But when she'd eaten
an aftertaste sweated
on Candy's skin
like mercy
coming out slowly
and later.

THE LAWFUL POSITION OF COAL

He's a self-contained solicitor
in a dark three piece suit and what we
have between us is nearly understood.
Along the esplanades his white head glistens.

And my mother at the tea dance says
she's proud not ashamed of being
a miner's daughter. She does understand
and won't come between us even if she could

but suddenly we're dressed in sacks
venturing out for a line-up from
the pavilion to the Winter Garden
beds where we see through grass, combed and glistening, long

and anaemic after days and weeks
of dark, nobs of coal rising, taking
over the surface. This isn't clearly
understood but the solicitor says he
accepts the fact that he was once tied at the neck.

THAT BOMB INSIDE US CRUISES L.A. 92

Where nothing internal
dies
down
there are sleepy days.

In the sun
a spark of live fur
on a sidewalk

Tom Waits wouldn't dream
of setting Staceys
on.

Cracks in the paving
tick tick tick
bars of a cage

pad pad pad.
200 psychos
therap in a single street.

A canned video rolls
from the door
of the Justice House.

At first
it's not what it looks:
a can of worms
with a kick.

MANTELPIECES

The Chinese have been whispering on the mantelpiece nonstop
since the Americans left them there two years ago.

There are often questions asked in the sitting room sometimes
rising to the level of argument but the two from China continue

murmuring quite unperturbed despite our approval-seeking looks.
They are deeper than the mirror under which they smoke and fan.

The elephant beside them, trumpeting in triumph,
that's why he's there, made out of English oak not ivory

shades them from the suddenness of our electricity
but Tom's pewter hip flask on the left is

as bashful as the moon while his service and
retirement dates stretch and ease across its modest face.

There is often snoring in the sitting room as smoke
slips up the chimney followed by a deathly hush

in which words of wisdom could be heard if it wasn't
for the travelling clock's tick tick tick, sneaking in.

JUNE

Just because I'm black
doesn't mean I like the heat.

And again she said it.
Black. Black,
surrounding it
with forgettable words
until I knew
she wanted me to say it

but I've never said I'm white.
To the mirror
I have been known
to say
You're washed out,
you've lost your colour, Mary.

THE OUTSIDE POOL

The all embracing clank of turnstile arms.
We're in. Between two skies air swims
with calls; shouts jump, splashed
by laughs from the deep.

Drawn to the edge, a vast sniff
of chlorine goes to our heads. it's
a sweet, cold world, a sundae. Blue
a measure of our happiness. The pool

an invitation card: Get totally immersed
for a moment or for ever.
We break the surface maybe a thousand times:
dip, dive and still don't know why.

We left the sea a long time ago,
learned to walk and came here
for our lifesaver's badge. Clifton,
Westminster rushes and in a sunburst

champagne springs to mind. A rich teenager
swivels like a fallen star, face down.
In love with incontinence
we stroke water all afternoon

until dead hands make for the side,
earned chocolate and a steaming mug.
The deckchair slackens. It's about five.
The attendant scoops leaves effortlessly;

stands back to watch Janet laugh at John,
in up to his thighs and screaming like an amputee.

UNCOMMITTED

It's
hard to say
'my'

grandfather
put his head
in the oven

without
taking a deep
breath.

DUCHAMP'S URINAL, 1917

Shockmounted to the level of art
the male side effect
for viewing not using.

    o pisstaker

He'd seen
look-alikes lined up against the wall,
got hold of one
and signed it.

Upended it's a female form:
recurring bride,
mother, her arms flowing
into old nurse.

    Mona Lisa tweaker

And for men who prefer men
it's a snowy cottage
in withdrawn light
or a surpliced boy,
a master piece.

    o

Once Duchamp did drop
the porcelain
for an exhibition
of amber streams

only to rehang
the readymade ego-breaker
over the dada door
with mistletoe for a

    kiss

WOMEN'S PLATFORM

The consignments: the deliveries
and dispatches continue all day.
We're hanging on a delivery of men.
God how we need them.
Mainly for dispatch of course
but while they're being processed
could be fun, particularly if
they come before the tears'
though not the light's delivery.
We're running out of that.
The shafts which catch the fox fur,
silver-line our coats,
are getting drizzley and the blocks
of it, needed on the platform
to spot the rise and drop of arms
are fainter by the minute. Men Day
is brilliant but I mustn't let
my arm get frenetic in case
my wave begins to ache. I'm O.K.
with the stuttering and halting
in my tracks. The trains help
with their ability to empathise.
I could do without the hats.
I'm sure they're a throwback.
Help with the tilt of course.
Flat shoes are going out.
They don't do much for the tilt.
There was a rumour yesterday
that handkerchiefs were coming back.

RESEARCHING UNCERTAIN GROUND, STANPIT MARSH

In the marsh
he meets water forget-me-nots
lady's smock
reeds censoring wind
listeners
for the songs of linnet and whitethroat
uncertainty.

The turf is fragile.
Some has been fenced off
for the effects of grazing to be assessed.
Green smudges his white boots.

Meanwhile a horse rolls over on Crouch Hill
innocently laying bare a patch of earth.

High tide maroons the horse
and an Early Bronze Age barrow
where a cremation urn and flint spears
were recently unearthed.
Sheep's sorrel turns the lips of the barrow red
and into thoughts of women.

It is written in the pamphlet that
all growth on the marsh is recorded.
Women pour out of the barrow
in stout shoes.

He jots down his first impressions
as the cormorants dry their wings
on Blackberry Point
and the tide turns.

SITTING ON THE MAP

Each path followed
its first foot
until they were woven:
feet and paths. And the threaders
nipped along for food,
a bit of he-ing and she-ing,
saw a hole in the hedge
or a badger
dead
on the edge of a fast lane
where the tension had gone wrong.

Carmen went right
on to a campsite
and met Ben. Together
they began to find a way
their path dividing each place.
At first some stasis was needed
– grass either side,
steady figures outside
their dream
to reach a door and settle in.

Others came
up the path:
a cooker, fridge, tele,
washing machine,
menders, letters, friends
and the porch stretched out.

Then Ben wanted a return
to old ways:
never the same place twice,
no tracks.
He bought a trailer
and called Carmen from the patch
she loved down at the allotments
where her thread was straight,
its passage near a neighbour's plot

a wary shuttle.

Ben was sitting on the map,
frowning at a score,
putting down his sax.

'Look at the crows Carmen,
their flight leaves no mark,
isn't worn.'

'Huh,' she gathered up
her pink geraniums,

held her tongue
till the first crossroad.
She turned in for the night
biting her old feather pillow
and left Ben studying AA Routes
for Motors into the early hours.

TRAILERS

Carmen suds up to her elbows
looking out over the old geranium

was as fetching as a promise made
in full view of a pay packet. It was

the pure white suds and arms cut off
like Venus said Ben. And nettles

weaving the trailer's wheels in the afternoon
relaxed. No one was going anywhere.

Flounces of geranium shook. Great cabbages
in choppy seagreen fields caroused,

caterpillars danced. 'Let's stay a while, put down
roots, Ben.' Potatoes jostled in their reaches,

turnips turned purple. The vegetables had
previous knowledge that it was not the way

of roots. A tin roof flapped and a bucket skidded
and rolled across the yard toyed by the wind.

A fork slipped, stopped and remained propped
for the moment against a corrugated sheet.

Ben and Carmen lay back sharing dope
and the yowling tom grew louder as he minced

across the yard, his swag drooling from his mouth.
'Cruel,' yelled Carmen who rose and threw

a dish of Prime Rabbit, then filled the kettle.
Ben got out his book of verse, spread

his hands across tableclcoth lanes. 'Let's
keep the feet of memory moving; scratch

a living like hens, two steps forward
one back,' he giggled, dropped a spoon.

'O.K. we'll leave a spade, a barrow, along the way.
Show we've made a path our home.'

He picked up the spoon and dropped the book.
'Don't be daft,' said Carmen

'we're in a rut and don't shake the geranium
darling. It's dead.'

STOCKPILING

A rabbit runs out
into the middle of the road.
I slow down, there's nothing coming.
He says my actions are
dangerous and sentimental but
as we round the corner
some idiot is careering
towards us trying to overtake.
Just misses us by seconds.
I give thanks to the rabbit.
He says we were very lucky.
No mention of the rabbit.
In silence I begin
to formulate a sentence.
The sentence when sharpened
will contain words like 'luck', 'your'.
'Rabbit' is redundant.
'Run out' might not be.

BEING ON A RING ROAD

It's late Friday afternoon
and I'm waiting to be served
at the Indian Stall on the corner
which will soon become a ring road.
They talk of easing somewhere else.
There's a queue tonight for beads,
essences and I want that blue-green
see-through scarf over there.
If I stand here long enough
maybe I'll fade and multi-coloured cars
will shoot through me. Perhaps one evening
a driver uncertain about his future
will miss me and I will become
a lucky sign or flicker of doubt.
Some time later he'll remind himself
his windscreen needs a clean.

BLUE GNOME

After jazz
in the middle of the night,
with a hundred miles to drive
I meet a fair
travelling the other way.

Creatures overblown
with static love are caterpillaring
towards me.

           Fantasy it seems
has no business travelling
in the light where
there's speed and reason.

A blue gnome's teeth
glisten above my head.
           What he finds
to laugh at will amuse him
until paint peels.

Snorting horses
articulate lost meadows
           and a ghost train
needing goggled escorts
                gains
involuntary followers.

ON THE ROAD TO ABERSOCH, ELECTION EVE 1992

At breakfast
in the middle
of so many real issues
William mumbles
through a mouth of cornflakes
'St. Christopher's your man.'

We leave him
dreaming in the garden
and drive away
down a finger of land
the kids used to say
pointed to old Ireland.

Gorse skims the lanes,
clads hills.
On the car radio
a hung parliament
is predicted just as
a yellow van appears

in the middle of the road
bellowing Vote Labour.
We swing over to the left,
pull in and check
our route.
Wrong again, we turn

around to chase
that stretch of sand
which once spread
like a buttered future.
There it is!
A brilliant day!

Driving back
up the hill
past Lloyd George's grave

– There's William
struggling across the river
waving daffodils.

HIGH TIDE

The flood
moves in, unruffled
though it could get tough.
The moon is making
suckers out of streets.

Water
runs right
across the road
without looking;
carries on regardless

ignores
policemen,
changes views
plays kiss-chase
with modest sandbags.

"He's got his clothes on!"
He dives in,
an oarsman beats the sea.
A skier from the stone bridge end
splits the estuary in two.

Sightseers
are ankle deep.
Camcorders whirr.
Outside Spar, Amy's wellingtons
are filling up.

Inside, the value's
flotsam-fresh,
the tide no time
for hygiene regulations
redeems Tin Fruit Island and jumps the queue.